Little Bear and Emily

WHAT A FRIGHT

A story of friendship ...

Text by Florence Ducatteau
Illustrated by Chantal Peten

PLURUS

'I am getting very tired moving all these rocks, Oliver,' says Emily.
'They are very heavy.'
'Shall we go and play cowboys and Indians in the woods, instead?'
says Oliver.

'You can be the indian and I shall be the cowboy,' says Oliver.
'OK,' says Emily picking up her bow and arrows. But poor Max is
left stranded on the rock in the water.

Emily is very good at sneaking up on Oliver.
'Where are you Emily? Are you there ?'

'Yes,' says Emily. 'Indians are always good at tracking,' says Emily.
'My horse is tired now,' says Oliver.' That's why you caught me.'

'Hands up, cowboy. You are my prisoner,' laughs Emily.
'Let's play a different game,' says Oliver.
He doesn't like being a prisoner.

'Let's play wolf hunters together. We'll be on the same side.'
'Cool,' says Emily. 'I'll like that game.'
The playmates start tracking through the woods looking
for the wolves.

'Oh, my goodness. These tracks are huge. It must be a monster,'
says Emily, looking around nervously.
Oliver tries to be brave. 'But there are two of us,' he says.

'But suppose the monster is very hungry? Maybe he hasn't eaten in two days. He might be the kind of monster which can kill us by looking at us,' says Emily, very scared now. The tracks they have found seem very big indeed.

'Don't leave me here, will you,' says Emily, nervously.
'No, and don't you leave me, either' says Oliver.
'We stick together, agreed?'
'Yes,' gulps Emily.

'Can we stop the game, now?' asks Emily. 'I am so scared.'
'OK,' says Oliver. 'It's time to go back and have tea now, anyway.'

'Emily?' asks Oliver, looking round nervously.
'Do you know where we are?'
'No I don't ,' says Emily, her voice quivering with fear.

'Don't worry, give me your hand,' says Oliver, trying to be brave.
'You are so brave, Oliver,' says Emily, holding his hand
and feeling better.

What was that noise?
'Something moved over there.'
'I am so frightened.'
'So am I.'

As it gets darker the two friends lose their nerve. It is so dark in the forest.

'Let's settle down here until it gets light. We'll try and sleep a little,' says Oliver, trying to comfort Emily. They both settle down back to back in a clearing surrounded by trees.
'I don't think I shall be able to sleep,' says Emily.

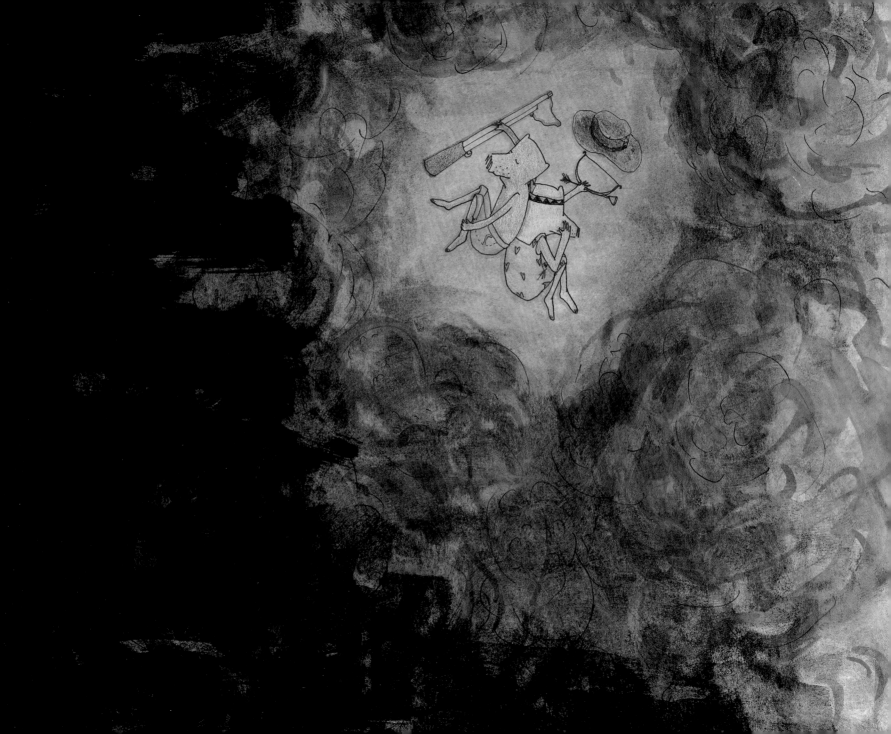

Morning has arrived and the two playmates wake up, slowly.
'Emily, look. Wake up. It's the hut. We are just by the hut,' says Oliver.

'So we weren't lost at all,' says Emily. 'That's a relief.'

Picking up their wooden horses, the two playmates go back to the
landing stage to find all their toys and to rescue poor Max from his rock.